Usborne First Experiences

The new baby

Anne Civardi
Illustrated by Stephen Cartwright

Consultant: Betty Root

There is a little yellow duck hiding on every two pages. Can you find it?

The Bunns

MOM BUNN

DAD BUNN

LUCY BUNN

SPOCK

TOM BUNN

BERTIE

This is the Bunn family. Lucy is five and Tom is three.
Their Mom is going to have a baby soon.

The Bunns' house

GRANNY AND GRANDPA BUNN

This is their house. Granny and Grandpa have come to look after Lucy and Tom while Mom is in the hospital.

The baby's bedroom

There is a lot to do before the baby is born. Mom and Dad are busy getting the baby's bedroom ready.

Lucy and Tom are helping too. Mom is painting their old crib for the baby to sleep in.

The baby is coming

Mom wakes up in the middle of the night. She feels the baby will be born soon.

Dad gets ready to take her to the hospital while Grandpa calls to say Mom is on her way.

The baby is born

SUSIE BUNN

The baby has just been born. It is a girl. Mom and Dad are very happy. They will call her Susie.

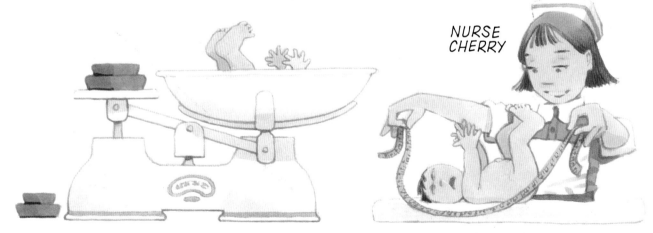

NURSE CHERRY

Nurse Cherry weighs Susie to see how heavy she is and measures her to see how long she is.

Susie is wrapped in a blanket to keep her warm. She has a name tag on her tiny wrist.

As soon as Dad gets home, he tells Lucy and Tom all about baby Susie. They are longing to see her.

Visiting the baby

The next day, Dad takes Lucy and Tom to the hospital
to see their Mom and baby sister.

Mom is in a room with other moms. They all have new babies. Which mom has twins?

Coming home

After a few days, Dad brings Mom and Susie home.
Everyone is excited and wants to hold the baby.

Susie is very sleepy. Mom is tired too. She will need a lot of help from Lucy, Tom and Dad.

Feeding Susie

When Susie is hungry, Mom feeds her with milk. Susie will need lots of feedings each day.

Bathing Susie

Now it is time for Susie's bath. Lucy loves to help Dad wash and dry her.

Going out

Mom and Dad, Lucy and Tom take Susie for a walk.
They are all very pleased with the new baby.

First published in 1985. This enlarged edition first published in 1992. Usborne Publishing Ltd, 83-85 Saffron Hill, London EC1N 8RT, England. © Usborne Publishing Ltd, 1992. First published in America in August 1994.